ROSALYN RABBIT RETURNS

by Elizabeth Crocker

Pictures by William C. Tobin

NIMBUS PUBLISHING LIMITED

Canadian Cataloguing in Publication Data

Crocker, Elizabeth J.

Rosalyn Rabbit returns

ISBN 0-920852-25-4

I. Tobin, William C. II. Title.

PS8555.R63R674 1984 jC813'.54 C84-098684-X
PZ10.3.C76Ros 1984

ROSALYN RABBIT RETURNS

Text copyright © Elizabeth Crocker

Illustration copyright © William C. Tobin

Designed by J. W. Johnson

Published by

Nimbus Publishing Limited

P.O. Box 9301

Station A

Halifax, Nova Scotia, B3K 5N5

CONTENTS

For Susan who used to think
she was a caterpillar. E.C.
For my parents, Rod and Jeanne
on their 40th Anniversary. W.T.

I
A SUMMER STORY

One summer day,

Rosalyn Rabbit slept in very late.

When she finally woke up,

she was very hungry.

She hurried outside

to have a breakfast of clover.

As she nibbled,

Rosalyn noticed it was very quiet.

She looked around for her friends;

they were nowhere in sight.

Then she saw a note

tacked on the tree stump

in the clearing:

"We waited and waited for you.

We've gone exploring. See you later.

Matilda Mouse, Deirdre Deer, Sam Sparrow,

Benjamin Bear, Charlie Chipmunk,

Susan Squirrel"

Rosalyn felt lonely
and wondered what she'd do all day.
Just as she was beginning
to feel sorry for herself,
she remembered she had another friend . . .
the little girl in the city whom
she'd met on Hallowe'en.
"I could go visit her."
Smiling to herself, Rosalyn quickly hopped
out of the woods and into the city.

When Rosalyn found her friend's house,

she rang the bell with her paw.

There was no answer and

no sign of the little girl.

Rosalyn sat down on the front step.

"Oh dear, now what will I do?",

Rosalyn moaned to herself.

Suddenly, Rosalyn heard noises
coming from the back of the house.
"I forgot . . . the little girl's
probably playing outside."
With that, Rosalyn hopped around
to the backyard.

The little girl was helping her mother
and her little brother was lying in the grass.
Rosalyn tapped the little girl's
foot with her paw.

When the little girl saw Rosalyn,
she squealed with delight.
"Oh, Rosalyn, I'm so glad you're here.
I have no one to play with today.
Can you stay and play with me?
We could play hide 'n seek or
tag or hopscotch or whatever you want."

"Hide 'n seek might be fun.

Do you think your little brother would like to play?"

"Well, he doesn't really know how to play.

He thinks he's hiding

if he covers his eyes.

Besides, he thinks he's a caterpillar,

not a child. Come see."

Rosalyn and the little girl walked over

to Peter who was lying in the grass.

Rosalyn put her nose close to Peter's face
and said, "Hi Peter."
Peter quickly replied,
"I not Peter. I soft caterpillar."
And with that,
Peter scrunched up his body,
just like a caterpillar,
and moved away through the grass.

Rosalyn wriggled her nose very excitedly.

"Amazing! Amazing!

Any idea why he thinks

he's a soft caterpillar?"

The little girl said, "Oh, that's easy.

He found a fuzzy caterpillar

last week and brought it home.

He kept patting it saying, 'so soft!'

I guess he fell in love with it

and decided to be one too."

"So does he spend his

whole day on the ground?"

"Well, he does act like a person sometimes,

but most of the time

he is scrunching or squirming

or trying to fly."

Rosalyn looked confused.

"What does flying have to do

with being a caterpillar?"

"Oh, he's practicing for the day
when he'll become a butterfly.
He saw a picture of a caterpillar
in one of my books and a picture
of a butterfly beside it
and my mum told him
that's what happens to caterpillars.

I wish he'd stop it

because then I could play with him.

Do you have any ideas, Rosalyn?"

Rosalyn was quiet for a minute

and then said, "I have a lot of friends

who are soft, fuzzy caterpillars.

Maybe I could get them to talk to Peter."

"Would you mind doing that, Rosalyn?"

"I can try. I'll go right now

and then we can play when I get back."

Rosalyn found most
of her caterpiller friends
hiding under the leaves
of their favorite bush.
She explained the problem
and asked them to help.
To save time
(because caterpillars are slow)
they all dropped on Rosalyn's back
and held on tight
as she gave them a ride into the city.

The little girl was sitting
on her front steps
and saw Rosalyn coming.
Rosalyn look very fuzzy!
When Rosalyn got to the little girl's house,
the caterpillars crawled off Rosalyn's back.
The little girl, Rosalyn and
the twenty-three caterpillars
went around to the backyard.

Peter was now busy jumping
off the sandbox trying to fly.
He squealed when he saw
all the fuzzy caterpillars.
He got down on the grass
and waited for them saying,
"I soft caterpillar, too.
I soft caterpillar, too."

The biggest caterpillar

lifted his head to speak.

"Hello! Rosalyn told us that you

think you're a caterpillar,

and not a little boy.

Well, it's nice to be a caterpillar

but we think it's better for you

to be a little boy.

First, caterpillars can't move very fast;

we can't chase balls

and run and play like you can.

Next, all we can eat is leaves;
we wish we could have spaghetti
and peanut butter and jam sandwiches.
Also, caterpillars often get squished —
by feet, by cars, by bicycles —
and that's no fun.

And anyway

we don't even get to become

beautiful butterflies."

"You don't, why not?" asked Peter.

"Because we become moths."

"Oh," said Peter.

"I not be soft caterpillar?

I not be butterfly?"

Peter waited a minute or two
and then stood up.
He looked a bit sad,
but all the caterpillars
crowded around his feet
saying, "Three cheers for Peter;
three cheers for the little boy."
Peter started to smile and
bent over to pat the caterpillars.
Then he stood up straight
and turned to Rosalyn and the little girl.
With a big grin on his face, he said
"O.K., I be Peter now . . .
but tomorrow I be hippopotamus."

II
A FALL STORY

One fall day,

when Rosalyn Rabbit was out for a hop,

she found a garden that

still had lots of carrots.

Rosalyn was very happy even though
she had to work hard
to drag the carrots to her house.
After all her work she was ready
for a yummy, crunchy, delicious carrot.
Rosalyn took a deep breath and
took a big bite of the nearest carrot.
Chomp! Her wonderfully sharp teeth
broke off a piece very nicely.

Seven bites later,

Rosalyn had reached the

thick end of the carrot.

Rosalyn opened her mouth wide

and chomped with all her strength.

The carrot was so big and so thick,

she did not bite through the carrot.

But worse than that,

her teeth were stuck.

Rosalyn wiggled the carrot

to try to get it free

and then the strangest thing happened.

When Rosalyn took the carrot

out of her mouth,

her teeth were still in the carrot.

She looked at the teeth and then

felt the space in her mouth

with her tongue.

Rosalyn was very surprised;

nothing like this had ever

happened to her before.

Rosalyn pulled her teeth out

of the carrot and

tried to put them back in her mouth.

She tried five times

and even used two paws,

but her teeth would not stay in her mouth.

Rosalyn started to wail and scream.

"Help! Help! Oh, no. Help! Help!"

Matilda Mouse was the first to arrive.

"What's wrong, Rosalyn?"

"Just look, Matilda.

My front teeth have come out,

and I can't get them back in.

I've tried five times.

Could you please try to

put them in for me?"

"Rosalyn, you can't put teeth back in

after they've come out."

"You can't?" wailed Rosalyn.

"Then, what am I going to do?"

"You'll have to wait for your
next teeth to grow in,"
explained Matilda.
"What 'next teeth'?
Do you mean I have more teeth in my head?"
Matilda nodded.
They're above the ones that came out."
"Well, will they grow in by tomorrow?"

Matilda laughed.

"Rosalyn, don't you know

anything about teeth?

No, they won't grow in by tomorrow.

It will probably take

a couple of weeks."

"Oh no, what am I going to do?",

wailed Rosalyn again.

"Rabbits needs their front teeth.

How will I be able to eat

all these wonderful carrots?"

Rosalyn made so much noise that the other
animals came to see what was going on.
Everyone tried to comfort Rosalyn.
Matilda rubbed her back,
Susan Squirrel offered to chew up
some of her nuts for Rosalyn,
Sam Sparrow said he would get
fresh worms every morning and,
Benjamin Bear offercd
to share his honey.

Rosalyn just shook her head.

"You're all very kind,

but you don't understand.

I don't like nuts and worms and honey.

I want my carrots and

I need my teeth."

Charlie Chipmunk had been very quiet.

He finally spoke,

"Why don't you go visit your friend

in the city?

Maybe that little girl would know

what to do about your teeth."

Rosalyn stopped crying and looked up.

"Good idea, Charlie.

It's worth a try."

Rosalyn wrapped her teeth in a leaf.

Using a long piece of grass,

she tied the leaf around her neck.

Carrying her two precious teeth,

Rosalyn hopped away towards the city.

When Rosalyn arrived

at the little girl's house

she saw her friend getting on her bicycle.

Rosalyn yelled, "Little girl! Wait for me."

The little girl turned and saw Rosalyn.

"Hi Rosalyn. I'm almost late for school.

Jump in my basket and come with me.

You can tell me what's new on the way."

Rosalyn was very excited
and very nervous about
riding in the bicycle basket.
In between gasps, giggles and squeals,
Rosalyn told the little girl about
her wonderful pile of carrots
and her two front teeth.
"I've got them wrapped up
in the leaf around my neck.
Matilda says I have to wait
for new teeth to grow in
but I can't wait.
Do you think you could put them in for me?"

"I'm afraid Matilda was right, Rosalyn.
You are going to have to wait
for your new teeth. Look at me."
The little girl grinned to show
two front teeth growing in.
"My front teeth came out weeks ago."
"But I can't wait.
How can I eat?" asked Rosalyn.

Rosalyn almost started to cry again

but they had reached

the little girl's school.

The little girl said,

"Rosalyn, I do have an idea,

but I have to go to school first.

If you can be really quiet,

I can sneak you in for the afternoon.

Jump into the pocket of my jacket."

In school, Rosalyn stayed as quiet
and as still as she could.
She even tried to slow down
the wiggling of her nose.
At one point, the teacher
asked the little girl
why she still had her jacket on.
Rosalyn was afraid she'd be discovered
but the little girl just said,
"I'm chilly and I forgot my sweater."

When the bell rang

at the end of the day,

the little girl leaned forward

and whispered, "O.K., Rosalyn,

we'll get my bike and go home now."

Rosalyn wasn't nervous about riding

in the bicycle this time.

She loved feeling her whiskers

pressed against her face and

the wind against her ears.

When they reached the little girl's house,

they went in the back door.

The little girl was careful

to wipe her feet and then yelled,

"Yoohoo, I'm home. Rosalyn is here, too."

Rosalyn heard the reply from upstairs.

"Okay, I'm just changing your brother.

I'll be down in a minute."

The little girl said,

"Now, Rosalyn, you sit down and watch."

The little girl got a bowl and

something else out of the cupboard.

The something else was shiny,

had holes in it and had four sides.

Then the little girl got a carrot
out of the refrigerator.

Rosalyn covered her eyes with her paws.

"I can't bear to see a carrot.

It makes me too hungry and sad."

"That's okay, Rosalyn.

You can cover your eyes if you want."

Rosalyn kept her eyes covered.

She heard a scraping sound.

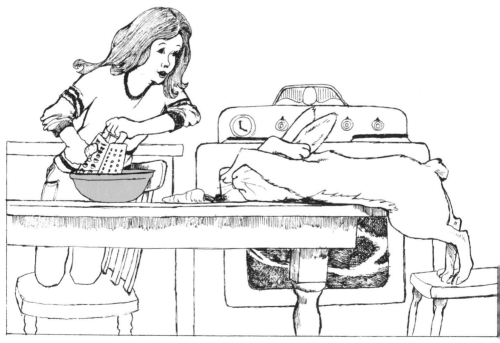

Then Rosalyn heard the little girl
put something on the table and say,
"Open your eyes Rosalyn."
Rosalyn peeked between her paws
and saw something orange in a bowl.

"It's grated carrots, Rosalyn.

I used the finest side of the grater

so it's really mushy.

You can just lap it up with your tongue."

Rosalyn leaned her paws on the table

and carefully licked what was in the bowl.

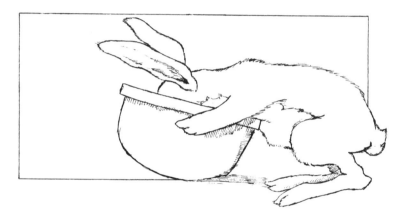

"Terrific! It tastes like carrot,

but I don't have to chew."

But suddenly the smile left

Rosalyn's face.

"I just remembered what you said . . .

that it will take weeks

for my new teeth to come in.

What am I going to do tomorrow?",

and Rosalyn started to cry

into the grated carrot.

"Don't worry, Rosalyn. I have an idea.

If you give me your teeth,

I'll put them under my pillow,

and the tooth fairy

will leave me some money. I'll take it,

plus some from my piggy bank,

and buy you your very own grater.

Then you can make your own carrot mush."

Rosalyn hopped across the table
to hug the little girl.
"I'm so lucky to have you for a friend."
Rosalyn gave her package of the two teeth
to the little girl.
Then the two friends just sat
at the table,
Rosalyn eating her grated carrot
and the little girl telling her
all about the tooth fairy.

III
ANOTHER HALLOWE'EN STORY

October arrived

and the leaves on the trees

began to turn yellow, orange, red and brown.

Rosalyn Rabbit realized

she had known her special friend,

the little girl,

for almost a whole year.

They had met on Hallowe'en night

when Rosalyn Rabbit had been dressed up

as a little girl.

No one had believed

she was in a costume

and so wouldn't give her any treats.

The little girl,

who was dressed as a rabbit,

had suggested that Rosalyn take her costume off.

Then the two "rabbits"

had gone from door to door.

The little girl's idea had worked

and they got lots of treats.

Rosalyn had told her friends in the woods

all about her Hallowe'en adventure and how

she had promised to go 'trick or treating'

with the little girl every year.

Benjamin Bear, Deirdre Deer, Charlie Chipmunk,
Sam Sparrow, Susan Squirrel and Matilda Mouse
had thought the whole thing
sounded very exciting.
When Rosalyn told them
Hallowe'en was soon approaching,
they all said,
"We wish we could come too, Rosalyn."

"That would be fun, but if you all came

maybe people would realize

I am a real rabbit

with real animal friends

and then wouldn't give us any treats.

If I just go with the little girl again,

people will just think

I am in a very good rabbit costume."

Charlie Chipmunk,

who seemed very wise, said,

"Maybe we could come into the city with you

but hide behind the bushes and just watch."

The animals started jumping up and down

and dancing, saying,

"Yeah, Charlie! Great idea!

We can't wait!"

When Hallowe'en finally came,

the animals were very excited.

Just before twilight fell,

Rosalyn Rabbit, Benjamin Bear, Deirdre Deer,

Charlie Chipmunk, Susan Squirrel,

Sam Sparrow and Matilda Mouse

went into the city.

Except for Rosalyn, the animals tried to stay

hidden most of the time.

When they reached the little girl's house,

Rosalyn rang the bell with her paw.

The little girl answered the door.

She had her rabbit costume on again.

"Oh good, Rosalyn, you remembered to come.

And look, my rabbit costume still fits.

My Mom said she made it big on purpose."

Suddenly the little girl noticed
the other animals hiding in the bushes.
"Rosalyn, you brought your friends!
How wonderful, but why are they hiding?"
Rosalyn explained. The little girl said,
"Well, it's going to be fun
knowing they are watching us."
"Is Peter coming with us?" asked Rosalyn.
"No, he's a little scared of
people with costumes and masks,
so he's just going to look out the window.
I told him we'd wave to him."
The little girl turned around
and yelled into the house,
"Rosalyn's here. I'm going now.
See you soon."

Rosalyn whispered to her friends,

"Okay guys, follow us but stay hidden."

The two rabbits decided to start

at the first house

they had gone to a year before.

The little girl rang the bell

and the two of them giggled

while they waited.

The same woman as before

opened the door.

"Oh Henry! Come here.

Remember those two cute

pretend rabbits who came to us last year?

They're here again.

My, how they've grown."

She gave Rosalyn and the little girl
some things for their treat bags.
Just before she closed the door, she said,
"Hope to see you again next year."
Rosalyn and the little girl
giggled and hugged each other.
"It still works! Let's try next door."

The two rabbits always showed their treats
to the animals.
Charlie Chipmunk, Sam Sparrow,
Matilda Mouse, and Susan Squirrel
were especially excited
about the things
they liked to eat —
peanuts, popcorn, and sunflower seeds.
Benjamin Bear and Deirdre Deer
had their eyes on a candy apple
that looked ever so delicious.

After a while, the little girl noticed
it was getting quite late
and said it was time to go home.
Rosalyn said she'd walk her home
before going back to the woods.
The two friends used the sidewalk
and the animals followed along
behind the bushes.

Rosalyn and the little girl
were so busy talking
they did not notice two very large ghosts
approaching them.
In fact, they would have bumped into them
if one of the ghosts hadn't spoken.
"Okay you little rabbits,
hand over your treat bags!"
The little girl said,
"But they are our treat bags, not yours.
You can't have them."

"Wanna bet little kid?

You don't look big enough to stop us."

"That's not fair," the little girl protested,

"You should pick on kids your own size."

"You sound pretty tough

for a little kid,

but not tough enough.

So hand over your bags

before we grab them from you."

Rosalyn and the little girl
hugged each other for protection
saying, "You can't have them.
We won't let you."
The two ghosts moved closer.
What the two ghosts did not realize
was that all the animals
had left their hiding places
and had snuck up behind the bullies.
Dierdre Deer and Benjamin Bear
had each gently taken a piece
of the ghosts' sheets
in their mouths.

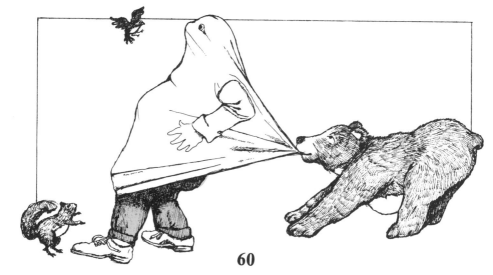

Just as the two ghosts

tried to grab the treat bags,

Deirdre Deer and Benjamin Bear ran,

with the sheets in their mouths,

in the opposite direction.

Meanwhile, Charlie Chipmunk,

Susan Squirrel, and Matilda Mouse

ran at the bullies' feet

making a huge racket

of chattering and squeaking.

Sam Sparrow flew around the bullies' heads

in tight circles.

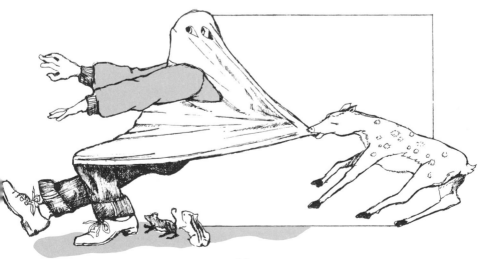

Rosalyn and the little girl

cheered their rescuers and laughed

as the two bullies screamed,

"Help! Help! What is this?

This is weird! Let's get out of here!"

And they went running off

as fast as they could.

The little girl turned to the animals.

"You were wonderful!

I'm so glad you were here.

Thank you for being so brave

and saving us."

Rosalyn echoed, "Me too!

I'm so proud of all of you.

I think we deserve

a Hallowe'en treat right now."

With that, all the animals spread out

one of the bullies' sheets and

sat down under a tree.

Matilda Mouse, Sam Sparrow

Charlie Chipmunk and Susan Squirrel

shared a package of sunflower seeds;

Benjamin Bear licked the candy off the apple

which Deirdre Deer and Rosalyn shared;

and the little girl ate

the largest chocolate bar she could find.

64